# 5-Minute
# BARNYARD TALES
## for
## Bedtime

**Illustrated by Peter Stevenson**

**Stories by Maria Buckingham, Nat Cato, Margaret Dixon, Selina Dowe, Nina Giglio, Susan Gilbakian, Tim Harrison, Wendy Hobson, Kay Jones, Dorothea Ralli, Clare Ronan, Anne Sharples, Karen Şimşec, Emily Smith, Zahra Tharani, Sylvia Turtle, Dennis Whelehan, Lin Wilkinson.**

**Derrydale Books**
New York • Avenel

Editors: Kim Kremer and Wendy Hobson
Editorial Assistant: Joanne Hanks
Production: Christine Campbell

Illustrated by Peter Stevenson

Stories by Maria Buckingham, Nat Cato, Margaret Dixon,
Selina Dowe, Nina Giglio, Susan Gilbakian, Tim Harrison,
Wendy Hobson, Kay Jones, Dorothea Ralli, Clare Ronan,
Anne Sharples, Karen Şimşec, Emily Smith, Zarha Tharani,
Sylvia Turtle, Dennis Whelehan, Lin Wilkinson.

This 1995 edition is published by Derrydale Books,
distributed by Random House Value Publishing, Inc.
40 Engelhard Avenue, Avenel, New Jersey 07001

Random House
New York · Toronto · London · Sydney · Auckland

A CIP catalog record is available from the Library of Congress

Copyright © 1995 Reed International Books Limited

ISBN 0-517-14054-3

Printed and bound in China

8 7 6 5 4 3 2 1

Felicity the little horse was fed up with all the other animals in the barnyard teasing her.

"You've got such long, wobbly legs," they laughed, "you'll never be able to enter the roller skating race at school."

Her mother bought her two lovely pairs of red skates – one pair for her front legs and one for the back. Felicity was very proud of them, but every time she tried to skate her legs got tangled up and she fell over.

"Keep on practicing," her father said from over the stable door. "You'll get the hang of it in the end."

The day of the race arrived. The principal, Mr. Rooster lifted the starting flag and they were off. Felicity was a little slow at first, but gradually her long legs took her past the leader and she won the race.

"See," she shouted, "long legs can be useful sometimes. Perhaps I'll be a racehorse one day!"

Farmer Robin hung his favorite old felt hat on a nail in the barn. He had worn the hat every winter for years. During the springtime, he hung it on the nail and only wore it on rainy days.

"I ought to throw it away and buy myself a new one," he said to himself, looking at the battered old hat. "But I'll keep it just in case."

As the days became warmer, Mr. and Mrs. Robin began to look for a place to build their nest.

"This is just the place," Mrs. Robin said excitedly when she found the old hat. Soon they had built a nest of twigs and lined it with soft feathers and sheeps' wool which had caught on the fences. Mrs. Robin laid six pale green eggs and proudly sat on them.

Once the eggs hatched, the robins were very busy. They flew in and out of the barn, bringing food to their hungry family.

Then one rainy day, Farmer Robin came to fetch his old hat.

"Well, bless my soul," he smiled. "That old hat hasn't outlived its usefulness after all." And he left the hat where it was for the robins to nest in every spring.

ason the pig couldn't contain his excitement. Today was a special day – he was going to have a birthday party!

The night before he had carefully decorated the house, checking that there were plenty of balloons. He had saved a blue balloon for his best friend, Sally.

The guests were arriving, but there was no sign of Sally. Then the phone rang, it was Sally. She wasn't feeling very well and couldn't come. Jason felt sorry for her and decided he would visit her after the party.

The party was great fun and everyone left with a balloon. Jason picked up Sally's and set off. On the way he tripped and fell. He let go of the balloon and the wind carried it away. Suddenly it stopped – on top of a black-berry bush. It was going to pop!

But no, Jason gently lifted the balloon off the bush and with a huge sigh of relief carefully wrapped the string around his wrist. Jason and the balloon arrived safely at Sally's house.

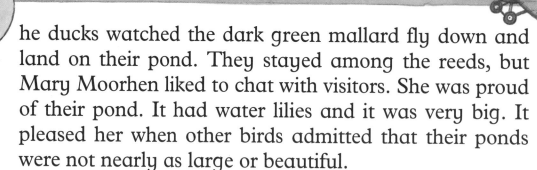

The ducks watched the dark green mallard fly down and land on their pond. They stayed among the reeds, but Mary Moorhen liked to chat with visitors. She was proud of their pond. It had water lilies and it was very big. It pleased her when other birds admitted that their ponds were not nearly as large or beautiful.

"Hello, I'm Mary," she chirped. "Welcome to our wonderful, big pond. Where are you from?"

"I'm Chuck," the green mallard said, "and I have just flown here from Canada across the most splendid, huge pond."

Mary was not happy to hear this. She swam around in a little circle, making ripples on the pond.

"Is that pond wider than this?" she asked.

The mallard laughed and stuck his tail in the air.

"Of course," he replied. "Much wider."

She pointed with her beak at the far reeds.

"Is it longer than that?" Again the mallard laughed.

"It is much longer." She pointed at the farm buildings on a distant bank.

"Surely it cannot be bigger than this?" she said.

"Silly thing," said Chuck. "I have flown over the Atlantic Ocean. It is so big that when you look at it, you can see no end and no beginning." For once, it was Mary's turn to be impressed, and she wondered whether she would ever see that splendid, huge pond.

Toby the tom cat was a typical farm cat. He had long claws and sharp white teeth that shone when he smiled. He swaggered across the barnyard by day, flexing his large tom cat muscles. All the birds and mice in the barnyard were frightened of him. He looked very fierce indeed.

But Toby wasn't really typical at all. In fact, Toby had a very unusual secret. Next time you visit the barnyard at night, when all the other animals are asleep, and you are very quiet, you might just hear a rather odd sound that goes TIPPETY TAP TAP.

For when night falls, Toby the typical tom cat likes to tap dance. Now that isn't typical at all, is it?

**B**ernard the chick was bigger than all the other chicks. He was also greedier and bossier. In fact, when they were really fed up with him, the other chicks used to call him Big Bossy Bernard.

At mealtimes, when the farmer's wife scattered the corn, Bernard would gobble up as much as he could, pushing the others out of the way and saying, "I'm bigger than you! I need more food."

One day he found a trail of corn running across the yard from a tiny hole in the farmer's wife's basket.

"I can have this all to myself!" he said. Greedily he ate the trail of corn, not paying attention to where he was going. Suddenly – BUMP! Bernard was knocked to the ground and peered up to see a great big goose looking at him crossly.

"Keep away from my corn," the bird hissed, pecking at him with its sharp beak. "I'm bigger than you! I need more food."

Bernard did not wait to argue. He was off across the barnyard as fast as his little legs could carry him. And after that, he felt a lot less "big" and he was certainly a lot less "bossy"!

**S**amson the puppy couldn't wait for spring vacation. "School's so boring," he said to his mother. "I shall have two whole weeks off. I'll play all day long, from the minute I wake up until the minute I go to bed. It'll be wonderful!"

On the last day before the break he came bounding back from school, his lunch box on his back.

"I'm home, Mom," he called. "Now I'm really ready to have some fun."

On the first morning of the holiday he chased the ducks and chickens, and swam in the stream in the afternoon. On the second day he followed the farmer's wife down to the village to do her shopping, and on the third day he watched the farmer making hay. But by the fourth day he was feeling a bit lonely – and *very* bored.

"When does school start again, Mom?" he said. "It's so boring at home. I can't wait for the end of vacation to see my friends again!"

Polly the cat liked living on the farm. Today she was especially happy, for her kittens were on their first outing. She led them out of the barn and into the sunlight. They looked around – timid but excited! Then they began to explore, staying close to their mother.

Joe was the bravest and wandered a little farther away. He saw Rachel Duck waddle past, followed by a trail of ducklings. They were little, fuzzy and brown – just like him. Joe thought they were another cat family.

"I'll follow them," he thought, joining the line. "This is good fun," he said, although he did find it rather hard to waddle like the ducklings.

When they came to the pond, Rachel hopped straight into the water, followed by her little ones. Joe followed them bravely. But he didn't float like they did and the water felt horrible! He jumped out and shook himself dry.

The ducklings were very similar – but they weren't the same as his family. He rushed back to the safety of his mom. He would never make that mistake again!

It was a hot day on the farm, so the animals decided to have a Fun Day.

Timmy Too Slow, the tortoise, got his name by being too slow at whatever he did.

Timmy entered the first race, but by the time he started to move forward, Rex had already won.

"Ha, ha, ha, Timmy, you are just too slow," the animals laughed.

At the three-legged race no one wanted to be Timmy's partner because they thought he would never win. He was awful at the egg and spoon race, and even worse at the sack race because he could not jump.

Mrs. Cluck announced that the last game would be statues and if anyone moved, even a little bit, they would be out.

Everyone tried to stand perfectly still, but they all dropped out, until only Timmy was left. He was just too slow.

**M**rs. Potawick was always grumpy. When it was hot, she complained of sunburn. When it was cold, she wanted the sun to shine. If the pigsty was muddy, she wanted it clean. If it was clean, she wanted to roll in the mud.

"Hello, Mrs. Potawick," said Matt the sheepdog one day. "Lovely weather today."

"It's far too hot," grumbled grumpy Mrs. Potawick.

"You've got nothing to grumble about," replied Matt. "I have to chase sheep all day."

Wilma the cow walked past on her way to milking.

"Hello, Mrs. Potawick. How are you today?"

"I'm tired and I've got a sore foot," she grumbled.

"You've got nothing to grumble about," replied Wilma. "The farmer is late with milking, I've walked all the way from the top field and my udder is full."

Later that day, Farmer Brown came and cleaned out the pigsty, leaving just a little mud in the corner. He washed Mrs. Potawick and gave her a good scratch in her favorite spot. He filled up one trough with food and the other with fresh water. Matt and Wilma passed the sty, expecting to hear her usual grumbles.

"Hello, Mrs. Potawick," they said. "Feeling better?" Mrs. Potawick opened her mouth to speak. But she could not think of a single thing to grumble about!

**B**obby the goat's dad could fix anything. Mr. Goat could fix clocks, radios, bicycles – you name it, he could fix it.

One day, Bobby was out playing with a big red balloon when the balloon landed on a rosebush thorn and burst. Bobby wasn't sad though – he knew his dad could fix it. He could fix anything.

"I'm afraid I can't fix it this time," said his dad, sadly. "Some things just can't be fixed." Bobby began to cry, but suddenly Mr. Goat said, "I know what I *can* fix though – your sad face, young Bobby." And with that, Mr. Goat gave Bobby a brand new red balloon and a big kiss.

Bobby was happy again – perhaps his dad could fix everything after all.

**J**effrey the pony had an old bicycle that needed painting. The trouble was that Jeffrey could not decide which color to paint it.

"Paint it green," said Sybil the sheep. "Grass is green and that's my favorite food."

"No, no, no," said Philip Pig. "Pink is best – pigs are pink so pink must be the best color."

"Blue!" cried Mr. Duck, "like the color of my pond."

"It must be yellow," argued Gertrude the chick. "Like my lovely soft feathers."

No one could agree, and Jeffrey was very confused. Suddenly, he had an idea and off he went with his paint-brush, without a word to anyone.

What a surprise when Jeffrey returned to show off his newly painted bicycle. Its handlebars were green, the pedals were pink, the seat was blue and the wheels were bright yellow.

Now everyone was happy!

**M**rs. Turkey was calling her chicks.

"Gobble, gobble," she said . "It's bedtime."

But Tilly Turkey wouldn't listen. She just carried on playing in the barnyard.

Mrs. Turkey held out her wing, and all the other chicks scrambled underneath. It was cozy and warm, and they were soon asleep. But Tilly Turkey just kept on playing.

All of a sudden, there was a rumble of thunder. Then came a flash of lightning. The rain began to pour down.

Tilly Turkey ran and hid beneath her mother's wing. All the other chicks were warm and dry, but Tilly was cold and wet. She woke them up.

They were so annoyed that they pushed her out into the rain again.

"Let me in," begged Tilly Turkey.

Mrs. Turkey felt sorry for Tilly. She lifted up her other wing so that Tilly could come in out of the rain.

"If you are lonely and wet, it's all your own fault," said Mrs. Turkey.

But Tilly didn't hear her. She was already fast asleep!

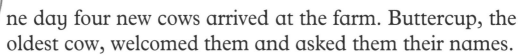

One day four new cows arrived at the farm. Buttercup, the oldest cow, welcomed them and asked them their names.

"Daisy," answered the first cow.

"Daisy," answered the second cow.

"Daisy," answered the third cow.

"Good heavens!" cried Buttercup. "Three of you all called Daisy! How very extraordinary. We'll have to call you Daisy One, Daisy Two, and Daisy Three!" She turned to the fourth cow. "Is your name Daisy, too?" she asked.

"Certainly not," said the cow with her nose in the air. "Daisy is a very *ordinary* name, and I am a very extra-ordinary cow. My name is Eglantine." And she walked away to the other end of the field.

What Eglantine did not realize, however, was that at that end of the field it was very muddy. One minute she was happily chewing clover – and the next she was stuck in the mud! Desperately she mooed for help.

"Quick!" said Buttercup, and the Daisies *were* quick. Daisy One caught hold of Eglantine by the tail, Daisy Two grabbed Daisy One by the tail, and Daisy Three grabbed Daisy Two by the tail. Together they pulled Eglantine out of the mud.

"Thank you!" said the frightened cow. "I'll never look down on the Daisies again. After all, I was rescued by a Daisy chain!"

**P**enny Pig's sty was the envy of all the other barnyard animals. It was warm and cozy and painted a lovely bright blue. But Penny still wasn't happy with her home. She wanted a view!

"It's no problem for you," she said to Hank the horse. "You're so big and tall you can see for miles from your stable door."

Hank thought hard about what Penny had said. He decided to surprise her with a solution to her problem.

The next day while she was out in the fields, he found a small wooden chair that had been left in the barn. He nailed it to the roof of Penny's sty. Next, he nailed an old piece of fencing to the chair to make a ladder.

When Penny came back she was thrilled! Sitting in the chair on top of her home she could see over the whole farm. She had a view at last!

**T**ommy Toad lived in a pond at the bottom of the farm.

"I wish I were not so ugly," moaned Tommy. "I am brown and crinkly and covered with bumps." He looked at his reflection in the green pond water and a large, wet tear slid down his crinkly brown cheek.

"No one will ever love me," he cried one day, as he swam sadly to the bottom of the pond and hid under a weed.

Lucy and her brother Tim were fishing in the pond. Tim caught Tommy in the bottom of his net.

"Look at this," said Tim. Lucy looked in the net.

"Ugh!" she said. "What a horrible, brown, crinkly thing." Tommy jumped out of the net.

"No one loves me," he croaked. "I am so ugly!"

But as he sank through the water he passed . . . another toad. She was brown and crinkly and covered with bumps.

"Hello," Tommy said. "I have not met you before."

"I am new to the pond," she said. "My name is Priscilla." Tommy's heart began to thump.

"I'm Tommy," he gasped. "And I think you're lovely." Priscilla blushed.

"Thank you," she said shyly. "You are the most handsome toad that I have ever seen." And they hopped off happily – the best looking pair of toads in the pond.

The most exciting part of the day on Acorn Farm was when Mr. Duck the letter carrier delivered the early morning letters.

Every morning, Glenda the donkey would trot down to the gate with the other animals to meet him.

"Is there a letter for me?" asked Glenda, hopefully.

"Sorry, not today," Mr. Duck would reply.

Day after day went by and poor Glenda never ever got a letter.

In the end, Glenda didn't even bother to ask – she knew there would be no letters for her. She just watched from her field sadly as the other animals collected their postcards and packages.

One day, Mr. Duck suddenly shouted, "Hey, Glenda! Don't you want your letter?"

Glenda's heart missed a beat. "For me?" she cried.

"Yes. All the way from Australia," said Mr. Duck.

Glenda tore open her letter. "It's from my sister!" she shouted. "She's coming to visit!"

And Glenda was even more proud when the animals all agreed that her letter was indeed the best letter ever.

**P**amela Pig lay on her back in the pigsty. She rolled over and over in the mud. She loved mud. Charlie Calf popped his head over the wall.

"Don't forget the picnic," he said. But Pamela just grunted. She knew her mother would make her clean herself up first and she couldn't be bothered.

"It's time to get ready, Pamela," said Gertie Goat.

"Baa-baa," bleated Lennie Lamb. "Picnic time!"

Pamela took no notice. She rubbed some mud on her tummy. She shook herself so it made lovely gloopy sounds. She would rather have fun being muddy than go to a picnic.

The barnyard grew quiet. Pamela's tummy rumbled. She thought of the others eating all the lovely picnic food. How she wished she had gotten ready in time!

A few raindrops splashed down, then more and more.

"I'm in luck!" Pamela shouted. The rain quickly washed away the mud. Soon Pamela was pink all over, from the tip of her pointed ears to the end of her curly tail. She waddled to the barn where the others were sheltered. Then the rain stopped and the sun came out.

"Come on!" Pamela cried. "Let's eat. I'm starving." They carried the baskets of food into the field and they all enjoyed a wonderful picnic.

**B**arnaby the bull was the largest animal on the farm. He was also the clumsiest. He didn't mean to tread on poor Christopher Cat's tail, it's just his feet were so big. He didn't mean to squash Daphne the donkey's chair when he sat on it – he was just so heavy.

One day while walking along daydreaming, clumsy old Barnaby bumped into Mrs. Hen's apple tree.

"Oh no!" cried Barnaby. "I've knocked all the apples off Mrs. Hen's tree. What shall I do?"

Barnaby was just thinking he might be able to glue the apples back on the tree when Mrs. Hen came hurrying out of the hen house.

"Oh thank you so much for picking all the apples, Barnaby. I was too small to reach them," she said. And Mrs. Hen baked Barnaby a huge apple pie that night as a reward.

**B**eryl Bee had been busy all day gathering honey from the flowers. Without noticing, she had wandered far from home. Beryl Bee was lost.

"Where am I?" asked Beryl. Looking around, all she could see were flowers.

Just then Chirpy Chicken came hopping by.

"I didn't know you lived on the farm," said Chirpy.

"I live in a beehive in the orchard," said Beryl, "but I can't find my way back."

"I'll show you the way home," said Chirpy Chicken.

Beryl Bee buzzed along behind Chirpy Chicken, and soon they reached the beehive. But a stray dog started to bark at Chirpy.

"I'm scared," said Chirpy.

"I'm not," said Beryl.

She buzzed around the dog's ears and settled on his nose. He had been stung once when he was a puppy, and didn't like it. The dog stopped barking and ran off.

"Thank you for rescuing me," said Chirpy Chicken.

"One good turn deserves another," said Beryl Bee. "Thank you for leading me back to the beehive. Won't you stay to tea? I've got lots of delicious honey."

How could he refuse?

Matilda was a tiny, furry kitten with cute pink ears and claws like needles. Each time little Susie tried to stroke her, she scratched her and spit.

One day, Matilda escaped from her basket and went to explore, looking for somebody to scratch.

First she met the horse. His feet were too big and hairy to scratch, so Matilda went on. The cows had fierce horns, so she avoided them. Next she saw ducks and hens who all had hard, snapping beaks, so she didn't try to frighten them either.

At last she found a creature who was even smaller than herself – a little mouse.

"Hello," said the mouse. "Are you new here?"

Matilda pushed out her claws and tried to look fierce.

"You poor little thing," said the mouse, kindly. "Don't be frightened. Have you lost your mommy?"

Matilda felt very silly, so she sat down and pretended to wash her face. Suddenly, she heard a loud "Mee-ow!" She looked up and there, towering over her, was an enormous striped tiger. Matilda was terrified.

Just then, Susie appeared and shooed the tiger away. "Naughty kitty," said Susie. "Come home. The big farm cats here are too fierce for a tiny kitten like you!"

Matilda curled up in Susie's arms and purred with relief. And she never spit or scratched Susie again.

**H**unker was a huge, bouncy puppy with enormous padded paws and a long tail which he wagged so hard that it sometimes knocked the farmer's two little boys right over. Timmy and Tommy did not mind a bit. They loved him, and often went to sleep in his basket with their heads on his tummy.

Their mother would see them and smile.

"People think Hunker's fierce because he is so huge. But just look at that softy!" she said.

One day a fox came to the farm to steal a chicken. Hunker bounded up to say "Hello," wagging his tail so hard that it knocked the fox to the ground. He stood over the frightened fox, grinning his puppy grin.

"Dad!" shouted Timmy. "Look, brave Hunker's caught a thief!"

"Keep still, or Hunker will eat you!" said Tommy, knowing perfectly well that Hunker was only playing. The farmer came and patted Hunker.

"Good pup!" he said. "You'll soon be a fine guard dog. Get up, you naughty fox! Hunker won't hurt you. But never take what doesn't belong to you again."

**M**rs Patsy Pig's young family had eaten their breakfast and were snoozing in the sty. It was midsummer and very hot.

"I'm going out for an hour to see an old friend," she said. "Please stay in the shade. Your skin is very pink and you're not very hairy, so you could get sunburned."

As soon as she was out of sight, Percy, the largest and naughtiest of the eight piglets, scampered over to the patch of sunlight in the middle of the sty.

"Come on," he called to the others. "It's lovely and warm here."

Soon all the piglets were having a super time chasing each other from the sun into the shade and back again. It was a very tiring game, and one by one they fell asleep – in the sun!

When Mrs Pig arrived home she found eight very sore piglets. "I told you to stay out of the sun, didn't I?" she scolded. "I hope you've learned your lesson!"

I shall be sorry to see this old thing go," said Farmer William, looking rather sadly at his old tractor as it stood at the side of the yard. "But it is just too old to be repaired any more. It will have to stay here until the scrap man can come and take it away."

Madeline the donkey overheard all this and it made her sad. The old tractor had rescued Isabel the cow from the bog. Bella the dog just loved to ride on the back behind the farmer, and the sheep watched for it on the coldest winter days when the farmer brought them extra hay for food. So she gathered all the animals together and they decided what they would do.

"I need somewhere safe to have my kittens," said Snowball. "I'll make a nest under the big wheels."

"I need a nest too," piped up Robin. "I'll build it under the seat."

"I can stretch out on the hood when I sunbathe in the morning," added Primrose Cat.

"And I can curl up on the floor when I'm worn out from rounding up the sheep," put in Bella.

Farmer William soon realized that he would not be able to move the old tractor even if he wanted to. But he was really rather glad!

**D**anny Duckling was gliding on the water in the duck pond when he noticed a strange, green creature swimming by.

"What a funny fish," Danny thought. He hurried off to tell his brother and sister, Derek and Dinah, what he had just seen. At that moment the green creature jumped out of the pond.

"Look! There it is!" Danny quacked.

"That isn't a fish. Fish don't jump," said Derek.

"Fish don't have legs, either," added Dinah.

So they went and told their mother all about it. But when Mrs. Duck saw it, she burst out laughing.

"You sillies! That's a frog," she said.

"Hi! I'm Frankie," croaked the frog.

"Why, the last time I saw you, you were just a tadpole wriggling beneath a lily pad," laughed Mrs. Duck. "Do come and tell me all your news."

"Would you like to play a game of hide and seek, Frankie?" asked Danny after a while.

"I'd love to, if you'll teach me," said Frankie.

Frankie learned quickly. He found good hiding places and his green skin made him hard to find. So they all played happily until it was time for lunch.

Charles had always been the biggest chick in the hen house, and he was becoming bigger every day. His legs were getting longer, his feathers smoother and he was growing a lovely red cockscomb on his head. He just could not wait to grow up!

"Soon I'll grow up and I'll make the loudest noise in the barnyard," he would tell everyone. Then he would throw back his head . . . and make a rather odd sort of clucking sound! Then the other chicks laughed at him.

"You'll have to be patient," his mother told him. "Soon you'll be making a noise that will fill the barn-yard from one end to the other."

One morning, Charles woke up earlier than usual, just as the dawn was breaking. He felt rather peculiar. He stretched his legs and strutted out into the yard. Then he climbed on top of the hen house, threw back his head and he crowed.

"Cock-a-doodle-doo. Cock-a-doodle-doo." The sound just flowed from his throat and he crowed and crowed. All the animals crowded round, chattering excitedly. Charles felt very proud. At last he had really grown up.

The farmer and his wife had a large pond full of goldfish at the end of their garden, next to the cows' field.

Todd, the old toad lived nearby. Sometimes he sat under the rocks in the shade where it was cool and damp, and sometimes he swam in the pond.

Goldie, one of the young fish, was having a birthday party, and she wanted all the farm animals to come, but of course, she couldn't get out of the water to ask them.

Todd, who was swimming in the pond that morning, had a brilliant idea.

"I can go over to the barnyard and tell them all to join us," he said.

That afternoon the farmer's wife looked out of her kitchen window and saw the sheepdog, the cat, the kittens, the piglets and the ducks sitting in a circle around the pond, and the cows and horses looking over the fence. What she didn't see was all the goldfish take a very deep breath and swim to the surface to sing "Happy Birthday" to Goldie!

**G**arth Goose was the grooviest bird on the farm. In his glittering boots, shiny leather jacket and shades, he cut a dashing figure, strutting his way across the farmyard.

"You other birds are so uncool," he would squawk. "Soaring above the clouds is not for me – flying is so old hat. And as for you chickens – you're always flapping about. Why don't you just relax?"

He did not like the duck pond either – he might get his head wet and spoil his fashionable hairstyle. No, Garth Goose preferred to while away his time playing his guitar and composing new songs for famous pop stars. But today, Garth was having problems.

"I just can't get the tune right," he said in frustration. Just then, a lark landed on a wall near Garth's head and began singing.

"That's beautiful!" Garth cried in astonishment.

By the evening, Garth and the lark had formed a great band with the chicken on drums and the ducks playing percussion.

"I was wrong about you other birds," said Garth, ashamed. "You sure are the coolest dudes a groovy goose like me could ever meet!"

**I**t was Dolly Duckling's birthday.

"I hope it rains," thought Dolly Duckling to herself. Dolly loved the rain. Her mom had promised her a birthday party, and all the ducklings on the farm had been invited. But the sun was shining, and Dolly Duckling felt sad.

"Nobody will come to my party," she said.

"Cheer up," said Mrs. Duck. "Perhaps it will rain after all. I'll ask the other animals."

So Mrs. Duck asked Jack Goat if it would rain that day, but he didn't know. She asked Delia Donkey, but she didn't know either.

Then Mrs. Duck saw Mrs. Cow lying down in the field. All the other cows were lying down, too.

"Why are you doing that?" asked Mrs. Duck. "Don't you feel well?"

"Cows always lie down when it is going to rain," said Mrs. Cow. "Everybody knows that."

"Thank you very much," said Mrs. Duck.

She told Dolly Duckling, who was delighted. That afternoon it rained and rained, and Dolly Duckling's friends came to the party and had a wonderful time.

"Clever Mrs. Cow," said Dolly Duckling.

**B**uttercup the cow sat under her favorite tree in the meadow with her mother, fluttering her exceptionally long eyelashes and painting her perfect little hooves. She was bored.

"There must be something more to life than eating grass and giving old farmer Haggarty his morning milk," she sighed.

"Nonsense, my lovely," mooed her mother. "Eating grass and giving milk is what we cows do best."

"Yes Mom, but *I* want to be special," said Buttercup. "Farmer Haggarty doesn't even notice me!"

The next day while the cows were being milked, a large black limousine drew up. The cow herd had never seen anything like it.

Suddenly, a rather fat man with a big hat and a cigar the size of a milk churn jumped out and pointed frantically at Buttercup.

"Oh those long eyelashes and pretty feet!" he exclaimed. "You're perfect for my new film. Come with me Buttercup and I'll make you a star!"

And do you know what? He did! Next time you see a cow on television, look carefully at the long eyelashes, the elegant hooves and the gleaming hide. You never know, it might just be Buttercup.

When Tiny was born he lay on the straw in the barnyard and gazed round him. "What am I?" he wondered.

He looked at the hens and ducks and geese and turkeys, but he hadn't any wings, so he wasn't a bird.

He saw a puppy and a kitten, but his legs were much longer than theirs and he didn't have claws.

Then he saw a piglet. It had a smooth twiddly tail and a flat nose, so he wasn't a pig.

Next came a cow. "That doesn't look like my mother," he thought.

He saw a ewe with her lambs but their coats were curly, so he wasn't a sheep.

Two horses passed. "That's better," he thought, until one of them gave a loud whinny, which somehow didn't sound right.

Then his mommy twitched her long, long ears and gave a great bray of pride for her new baby. She pushed her nose under his soft furry tummy to help him to get up on to his long wobbly legs and said lovingly, "Come on little donkey."

**B**ingo lay sleeping in his lovely new kennel. It would be hours before Carl the rooster would be waking up the barnyard. Suddenly he awoke with a start! The hens were making a dreadful noise – squawking and flapping, scratching and rustling in the hen house.

He sniffed the night air. He could smell a fox!

He rushed round to the back of the hen house, barking loudly. There was the wild fox, digging under the wire fence, trying to get into the house. Bingo ran up, barking and growling so fiercely that the fox ran off with his tail between his legs. He was so frightened he would never return to this barnyard again.

Farmer Tom ran up, wearing his pajamas with his bathrobe flapping and his work boots on the wrong feet. He saw at once what had happened.

"Good boy, Bingo," he panted, patting Bingo's head. "Back to sleep now, old boy. He won't bother us again."

When Bingo woke again next morning, he sniffed the morning air. Outside his kennel there was a large juicy bone – a reward from Farmer Tom.

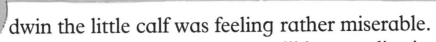

**E**dwin the little calf was feeling rather miserable.

"When you're bigger you will have to live in a field on your own and be fierce and chase people," his cheeky twin sister told him.

"But I don't feel fierce," Edwin said. "I want to be friends with everyone. And I *don't* want to live in a field all by myself."

But as time went on his mother had another calf, and the farmer had to find a new field for Edwin. However, he had a kind heart and knew how gentle Edwin was.

"We usually put a notice up on the field gate saying 'Beware of the bull'," he said. "But I don't think we need to do that with you, Edwin. How about sharing a field with old Peg the donkey? She'll keep you company and she's good at telling stories."

Well, Edwin was so pleased the farmer didn't even have to lead him down to the field. He trotted right in front of him, mooing softly, down the lane to Peg's field!

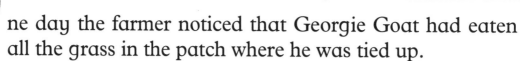

One day the farmer noticed that Georgie Goat had eaten all the grass in the patch where he was tied up.

"That gives me an idea," said the farmer. So he moved Georgie to the front garden of his house, and tied him to the fence.

"Now Georgie Goat will eat all the grass in my front garden, and I won't have to mow it. Georgie will save me lots of work."

And that is exactly what happened. Georgie began to eat the grass. Later that day the farmer's wife hung her clean washing on the line.

"It's a warm, sunny day," she said. "My washing will soon be dry."

But when she went back to collect her washing, it was all dirty again. Georgie Goat had butted it with his head, knocked it on the ground, and trampled all over it. He had even eaten two pairs of socks!

"Georgie Goat may have saved you a lot of work," said the farmer's wife to her husband, "but he has made an awful lot more for me!"

**E**leanor the sheep was frantic. Where could her lamb have gone? She had only turned her back for a moment, she told Patrick the goat, and Lily had disappeared.

Patrick was a practical fellow.

"Don't worry, my dear," he said. "I have an idea," and he ran to where Rover was sleeping in the sun.

"Quickly," he said, shaking Rover to wake him. "You must find Lily Lamb. She is lost."

"But I'm a sheepdog," complained Rover, "not a bloodhound. I don't think I can find her."

"Nonsense," replied Patrick. "You can do it."

Rover was not so sure, but he was kind and always did his best. He began to sniff the ground, moving this way and that like a vacuum cleaner on a carpet.

Suddenly Rover took an extra large sniff and then began to weave his way across the field, through a hole in the fence and into the next field. They waited.

Then, from what seemed a long way away, there was a bark, and very soon another bark and a tiny bleat as Rover chased little Lily back to her mom.

"I told you that you could do it, old man," said Patrick. "You can feel very proud of yourself."

"So you did," smiled Rover – who felt as proud of himself as the others did.

Dorothy sat sadly at the edge of the barnyard. She felt very alone without her mom.

"If only I could fly," she sobbed to Peter Pig, "I could look down and I'd be able to see her."

"I'll teach you to fly," said Peter hopefully. "I'm sure you only have to flap your wings." Dorothy tried, but her tiny, soft wings were just too small.

"Jump off the fence and flap your wings harder," encouraged Peter. The little bird hopped onto the fence and flapped. For a moment she hovered, then she crashed to the ground.

"One last try," said Peter. "Climb up the oak tree and jump off – and flap your wings really hard." Dorothy did just that – and rose high into the air! Peter was delighted. Then suddenly, Dorothy dropped like a stone into the pond and disappeared!

"Oh no! Where are you?" Peter wailed, peering into the water. But then he heard a voice cry, "Look, Peter. I've found my mom!" Peter looked up. There was Dorothy paddling in the water with a family of ducks. She may not be big enough to fly just yet, but she could certainly swim!

"Today we're going up to the hills to graze," the mother sheep told her lambs one spring day. "Make sure you follow each other's tail or you might get lost."

Jed the sheepdog rounded them up and the farmer led the way. Lester, one of the lambs, had other ideas, however. Halfway up the steep track he thought he'd skip off and explore on his own.

"Come back here," his mother and sister called, but he wouldn't listen. After a few minutes he looked around and couldn't see the others anywhere.

"Oh no," Lester wailed, "I wish I'd listened to Mom."

Just then, over the top of the hill, he saw Jed racing towards him. For once Lester was glad to see the bossy sheepdog.

"Come on," Jed barked. "Sheep always follow each other. You didn't, and that's how you got lost!"

Tracy was a very pretty sheep.

"Do look at my lovely curly coat," she said to her brother Jason. "I am so beautiful!" she baa-baa-baaed.

"You are very pretty," said Jason, "but I do wish you would stop telling everyone about it!"

"Look at me!" Tracy said to Pudgy Pig. "Have you ever seen a finer sheep in all your life?"

"Yes, yes, very fine," grunted Pudgy patiently.

Soon the spring came and the weather grew hotter.

"Time to shear the sheep," said Farmer John. "We will use their coats to make cardigans and jumpers."

"Not me!" said Tracy. "My coat is much too fine to be cut." She pleaded so hard, with tears in her eyes, that eventually the farmer relented.

"Very well, Tracy," he said. "You may keep your coat, but I don't think you'll thank me for it!"

The summer came. The sun was hot and bright.

"I feel so hot and sticky," moaned Tracy. "I do wish I could take my coat off!"

"I thought you wanted to keep it," smiled Jason.

"I did warn you," chuckled the farmer.

"I am silly," admitted Tracy. "Next spring, I'll be happy to be sheared like all the others."

# PRUDENCE IN THE SUN

**E**verybody on the farm loved the summer. When the sun shone brightly, all the animals could be found sunbathing and playing volleyball in the barnyard. Everyone except Prudence the pig. She had to stay indoors because she got such terrible sunburns.

"It's not fair," she thought to herself. "The other animals have wool or fur to protect them, and when the ducks get too hot they can go for a swim to cool down."

The animals felt very sorry for Prudence. Suddenly, the swallows said they had an idea. They began flying back and forth collecting straw and weaving it together. The farmyard animals watched them and wondered how building a nest would help poor Prudence. But when the clever swallows had finished, their friends saw that it wasn't a nest they had been making but a beautiful big straw hat!

Now whenever Prudence goes out into the sun, she wears her hat to keep her in the shade and never gets sunburned any more.

Cheeky was Molly Hen's naughtiest chick. One day he was playing hide and seek with his new friends, Paddles and Emmy the ducklings. It was great fun, rushing and quacking and clucking in and out of the long grasses. Soon they heard Clara calling her ducklings for lunch.

"See you, Cheeky," they said, swimming happily off across the pond. Cheeky watched them.

"That looks like fun," he thought, and paddled off after them into the pond. The water was cold where it soaked his feathers but Cheeky went still deeper until suddenly he found himself sinking. He had never been so frightened! Then he felt something hard and firm nudge him back on to the bank. It was Clara, pushing him out with her beak.

"You silly chick," she said, ruffling his wet feathers. "Only ducklings can swim, my dear, not chicks." Molly clucked over and snuggled him safely under her wing to dry in the warmth.

"I don't think I'll try swimming again," said Cheeky, and they all laughed.

"Charlie, you're late again!" said the teacher when Charlie the rabbit arrived half an hour late for school for the third time that week.

"I'm sorry, Sir," said Charlie.

"What you need is an alarm clock," said the teacher, and he was right.

So when school finished that day, Charlie went to see Mr. Pig the shopkeeper. "I want to buy the loudest alarm clock you have," said Charlie.

The next morning, the alarm clock's loud bell woke Charlie up with a start.

"Hooray!" shouted Charlie. "Today I won't be late!" He quickly got dressed and ran to school.

"I'm half an hour early today," said Charlie to the teacher when he arrived.

"Well done, Charlie," said his teacher. "But it's Saturday – there's no school today."

Poor old Charlie *was* embarrassed.

"But never mind," said the teacher. "At least you were early today." And he gave Charlie a big vanilla ice cream cone as a reward.

**I**t's mine," shrieked Flim.

"No, it's mine," screamed Flam. All the other hens huddled at the other side of the hen house and covered their ears with their wings. Flim and Flam were making a dreadful din. Roger the rooster tried to ignore them, hoping they would get tired and stop arguing. But they only became noisier.

"What's up with you two?" he crowed.

"She's stolen my egg," said Flim.

"No, she's stolen *my* egg," said Flam. Roger watched as each hen tried to sit on the same egg by pushing the other one off.

"Stop doing that or you'll break the egg," he cried. Flim jumped up quick as a flash and said, "Oh. I hadn't thought of that." But Flam sat down on the egg and said, "I don't care. It's mine. I can do what I like with it."

Roger cleared his throat, "Cock-a-doodle-doo," and said, "Flam, get off that egg. Flim cares about it more than you, so from now on it belongs to her."

The hens cheered, "Wise Roger!" and settled down onto their nests for a peaceful sleep.

# THE MER-PIG

**S**ometimes Edward Seagull would stop by the pig sty. If he was in a good mood, he would tell tales of the sea. Pepper loved to listen. She would gaze at the gull, eyes glowing, listening to his stories of exotic places.

One night, after a visit from Edward, she thought she heard a voice in her ear. "Swim, swim," it said.

"I can't!" said Pepper. "Anyway, I'm not in water."

"Try," said the little voice.

Pepper kicked her trotters, and found to her surprise that she *was* swimming – and the water *was* salty! She turned to see a little piglet about her size – with a fish's tail! She could hardly believe it.

"I'm a mer-pig," said the creature. "I'm going to show you around under the sea. You'll be safe with me."

Together they explored beneath the waves, swimming with the fish and sending surprised crabs scuttling across the sea bed.

"I must take you home now," said the Mer-pig. "But keep this shell to remind you of your magic adventure."

Next morning Pepper woke up in her straw bed. She could not wait to tell her family about her adventure.

"Don't be silly!" they scoffed. "There's no such thing as a mer-pig!" Pepper held her shell tightly. She knew that the magic adventure had really happened.

**G**raham the turkey was given a bright red sled for Christmas. It was the first time he had ever seen one.

"Wonderful!" he gobbled excitedly. "But what is it for?" he asked his mom.

"Well dear," Mrs. Turkey explained. "You carry the sled to the top of the hill and sit on it. Then you slide all the way to the bottom."

"Wow!" said Graham. "Thank you, Mom," and off he went to try it.

An hour later, Graham returned, puffed out and rather angry.

"It doesn't work!" he said.

"Oh you silly turkey," his mom laughed. "You need to wait for the snow first!"

The next morning, snow fell all around the farm and Mrs. Turkey took Graham and his sled right to the top of the hill again. This time when Graham sat on his sled the slippery snow made the sled slide.

"Wheeee!" he yelled, all the long way to the bottom.

**M**ary's pony, Tubby, was very small and very round. He was her first pony and she loved him dearly. But now when she rode him, her feet almost touched the ground!

"We must do something about that pony," Dad said.

A few weeks later, it was Mary's birthday. She woke up very excited and looked around the room. But there was not a present in sight! Slowly and sadly, she got dressed. Reaching for her boots she noticed a scrap of paper attached to some yarn. "Follow me," it said.

So she followed the yarn down the stairs, into the yard and to the stables. There she found a lovely new pony.

"Surprise!" said Mom and Dad. "His name is Thunderbolt. Happy birthday!"

"Dad, he's fantastic," gasped Mary. "Look at his long legs and his silvery mane!"

They saddled up Thunderbolt and Mary mounted his back. At once, he set off across the yard and into the field. Tubby watched the activity. Mary did not even look at him. His head drooped.

"I only have stumpy legs and a stubbly mane," he said sadly. But Thunderbolt was going too fast.

"Help!" cried Mary. Thunderbolt stopped dead at a hedge and Mary was thrown with a bump. She started to cry. Tubby trotted up and licked away the tears.

"Oh, Tubby, you are so kind and gentle," she said. "And I did not even pat you today of all days. However big I grow, you will always be my favorite."

**W**hat's on the other side of the fence?" asked Lewis.

"You'll find out when you've grown up a bit," his mother replied. "Don't be such a nosy lamb!"

But that answer didn't satisfy Lewis. He wanted to know NOW!

He asked the goats and the ducks. He even asked the snooty geese, but no one would tell him.

"Okay!" he thought angrily. "I'll just have to find out for myself," and off he walked. In the corner of the field someone had left an old mattress.

"Great!" thought Lewis. "A trampoline!"

He jumped on to the mattress and began to bounce higher and higher. "Now – I – can – see – over – the – fence!" he panted.

Suddenly he felt hot breath on his face. Lewis was eye to eye with the biggest, ugliest and fiercest bull on the farm! He fell back onto the mattress with a thump.

"I think I'll stay on this side of the fence until I'm a bit bigger," he told his mother.

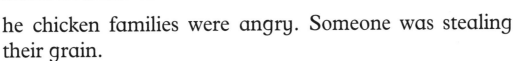

The chicken families were angry. Someone was stealing their grain.

"We must organize a patrol," said the Colonel, who was the oldest rooster on the farm, "and keep a night watch to catch the thief!"

Later that night, the Colonel and his eldest son were patrolling up and down the farmyard when they heard a scratching noise coming from behind the bags of grain.

"Quick!" hissed the Colonel. "The thief's over there!"

They ran over to the bags, pulled them out of the way and the Colonel shone his torch into the corner. Sitting, blinking in the bright light, was Heather Hen, munching her way through a large bowl of grain.

"But I'm so hungry!" Heather cried. "My older brothers always get to the food before I do and there's never any left for me."

The Colonel took Heather back to her parents, and they promised her that she could have her very own bowl of grain from then on.

**K**imberly the cow was fed up eating grass all day, especially when the farmer's strawberries looked so red and juicy. So she tiptoed across the barnyard and nibbled a few strawberries while no one was looking.

The next day the farmer was hopping mad.

"Look at my strawberry patch," he cried. "You've trampled on it and turned my strawberries into mush."

The farmer picked up all the crushed strawberries and put them into a bucket to make strawberry jam. Then he went into the farmhouse to wash his hands. Just then his wife came out and started to milk Kimberly. But she forgot to look inside the bucket and squirted Kimberly's milk right on top of the mushy strawberries!

When she had finished milking Kimberly, the farmer's wife looked into the bucket and screamed! The farmer ran out to see what all the fuss was about.

"Look," said the farmer's wife, "Kimberly has eaten so many strawberries she's made strawberry milk shake!" The farmer laughed and laughed! And when he explained what had happened his wife laughed too. And as for the milk shake – it was delicious!

**E**veryone in the pigpen was fast asleep – except Pickle. As soon as the sun came up he squealed, "It's my birthday. Wake up everyone. Wake up!" But everyone stayed fast asleep, so Pickle squeezed under the pigpen gate and escaped into the barnyard to find a friend.

First he met Henry the horse, but Henry trotted past in a great hurry. Next he met Mandy the hen, but she rushed out of sight without even saying hello. Then he met Chloe the lamb, but Chloe skipped past without stopping.

Pickle turned back home, his tail drooping between his legs. "No one cares about my birthday," he said to himself. But when Pickle arrived back home to the pigpen it was empty! "Hello, anyone there!" he called. No one answered.

Suddenly Henry, Mandy, Chloe and all the pigs jumped out from nowhere and shouted, "Surprise, surprise. Happy Birthday, Pickle." Pickle felt happy again!

**B**arney, the farm dog, was sleeping peacefully by his kennel in the corner of the barnyard. His snoring was so loud he didn't hear the tiny ducklings, Mark and Lizzie, creep over to where he lay in the shade. They had decided that Barney's huge water bowl was just what they needed on this hot summer's day – their own private swimming pool!

They slipped over the rim of the bowl and into the lovely, cool water. Bobbing and diving, splishing and splashing, they were so excited chasing each other around they didn't notice that Barney was beginning to stir and stretch.

"Aaaahh!" Barney yawned. "Time for a drink. My mouth is so dry!"

With a big slurp, Barney dipped his tongue into the water bowl. "Erggh!" he spluttered. "I almost swallowed those furry lumps." Mark and Lizzie got a terrible fright!

Barney carried the two ducklings back to the farm pond sitting on his head.

"That's the last time you go swimming in my water bowl," he said.

The kittens' bedroom was in a dreadful mess again. Their clothes were in a pile by the door, they had spread paintings on the floor to dry, and there were so many toys and books on the carpet that it was hard to find any clear space to walk on.

Poor Clara Cat didn't know what to do. How could she persuade her kittens to keep their room tidy?

Today they were going to Tanya Turkey's birthday party. They were going to wear their new blue dresses, which had pink ribbon threaded around the sleeves. The kittens loved them – but they couldn't find them anywhere. They looked and looked but their room was so messy it was almost impossible to find anything.

Just then they caught sight of the pink ribbon underneath a pile of books. They pulled – and the jar of dirty water they had been painting with tipped all over their new dresses.

"Now you know why it's important to keep your room tidy," their mother said. "You'll just have to go to the party in your old dresses." From then on the kittens kept their room tidy – well, most of the time anyway.

**I**t was Farm Fun Day and the wheelbarrow race was about to begin. Six wheelbarrows were lined up at the starting line and the first team to push their barrow to the fence would win a huge jar of candy.

The duck team were sure they would win as they had been practicing for weeks. But they didn't know that the pig's team had a secret weapon – tractor grease – which they had spread along the race track.

The race began and all the animals began shouting for their favorite teams. The ducks' barrow was soon in the lead, when – DISASTER! Their barrow hit the patch of grease and went skidding into the pond. The grease patch had spread across the barnyard and the pigs also ran straight into it. Squealing loudly, they too went headlong into the pond.

The goats who were judging the race declared that no one had won and no one had lost. So the pigs apologized for trying to cheat and cleared up the huge mess they caused and the jar of candy was shared between the teams.

One day a strange-looking animal appeared in the barn-yard. Everyone clustered around the newcomer and stared. Gary the goat, who wasn't scared of anything, moved to the front of the crowd. He cleared his throat and said loudly, "So who are you?"

"I'm Jane. I'm a guinea pig," said the stranger.

"She doesn't look much like a pig to me," muttered one of the geese.

"I live in the house down the road, but I'm fed up with our tiny garden," said Jane. "Could I stay here?"

"Can she live with us, Mommy?" one of the piglets squealed, jumping up and down.

"I think your mommy will be worried about you," the mother pig said kindly. "Stay for some tea and then – we'll see."

Jane happily settled down to share the piglets' tea. Meanwhile, Mrs. Pig sent Gary to bring Jane's mom down to the barnyard.

It was starting to get dark as they arrived. Jane was beginning to wonder whether she wanted to stay in the barnyard after all. She felt rather small.

"I think visiting is best," she said, as she snuggled up closely to her mom on Gary's back for the journey home.

The young farm animals were putting up their tents in Bluebell Wood. They were on a camping weekend with their school teacher, Mr. Gander.

They gathered around the camping stove and dug into big plates of potatoes and beans. After they had eaten, everyone took turns telling a story. Some of the tales were very scary – all about ghosts in the woods.

Later that night, Mr. Gander thought he heard some noises. He poked his beak through his tent flap and saw a very strange shape sticking out of the hens' tent.

"Who's that, who's that?" he shouted and ran over, flapping his wings.

Brian, one of the cows, was trying to get into the hens' tent, but he was stuck in the zipped flap which wouldn't open wide enough to let him in.

"I was scared of the ghosts," he explained to Mr. Gander after he had been rescued, "And I thought it was your tent."

"Well, you're safe now," smiled his teacher. "I'll keep watch for any ghosts!"

Owen the pig looked over the wall of his sty.

"Yum! Yum! Yum!" he said. The tree by his sty was full of big rosy apples. Some of the apples had fallen onto the grass.

"If only!" sighed Owen. "If only I could get out of my sty and eat some of those juicy apples!"

"Dinnertime, Owen!" shouted Sally the farmer's daughter. "I have brought your pig feed and scraps from the kitchen. There's potato chips, porridge and cornflakes! All your favorites!" Owen poked his long pink snout in his trough.

"Huh!" he snorted. "I am fed up with scraps!" . . . but he gobbled and slurped and snorted and ate them all up just the same.

Then Owen noticed Sally had left the latch off his gate. He pushed the gate gently with his trotter. The gate fell open!

"Yippee!" said Owen as he scurried over to the bottom of the apple tree.

"Yum! Yum! Yum!" he snorted with delight as he gobbled up the juicy red apples.

But . . . oh dear! . . . What a terrible tummy ache he had that night!

One day when Annie the hen was out walking, she came across a large egg hidden in the hay.

"I wonder who this belongs to," she thought. Since no one seemed to want it, she decided to sit on it. The other hens told her she shouldn't sit on strange eggs, but Annie ignored them. She sat on the egg for a very long time and looked after it carefully.

One day she felt the egg moving beneath her. She jumped up, and as she watched, the egg cracked and, slowly but surely, out came a tiny and very hungry chick.

Annie fed her chick big, juicy worms, as many as she could find. But still the chick was hungry. She had a huge beak and swallowed the worms whole. She grew bigger and bigger. When she was almost as big as Annie she started flapping her wings. Annie couldn't teach her to fly because she did not know how.

"Oh dear," sighed Annie, "what am I to do?"

Then she had an idea. Perhaps her friends at the pond would help. So Annie led the chick down there. When the ducks saw the chick they quacked and quacked! Annie saw her mistake at once. The chick was, in fact, a baby duck! She gave Annie a big hug.

"I'll come back and visit you soon," she called, as she swam off happily with the other ducks.

**D**an and Dennis, the black and white calves, had been pestering their mother all day asking if they could sleep in their little tent that night.

"Oh please," they begged – again, "it's a lovely warm evening, perfect for camping."

"Very well," their mother said, "let's see how you get on tonight."

So after tea Dan and Dennis put the tent up in the field next to their barn. Then they snuggled into their sleeping bags and settled down for the night.

At home they were usually asleep as soon as their heads touched the pillow, but tonight they just couldn't sleep. It was very dark, and they heard funny noises which sounded like ghosts howling, not like the soft moo-ing of the other cows at night.

Just then their mother popped her head through the tent flap.

"Are you all right?" she said.

"Yes," said Dan and Dennis together, "but perhaps we'll come back into the barn. We'll camp out another night."

**H**erbert, the old sheepdog, lay in the sun, snoring.

"Get up, Herbert!" shouted the farmer. "The sheep have to be rounded up and put in their pen."

"Go away," barked Herbert.

"Come on, lad," encouraged the farmer, tugging at Herbert's collar.

"Please go away," growled Herbert. "I am comfortable lying in the sun and I do not care any more about those silly sheep."

"What a lazy dog you are," said the farmer crossly. Then he thought for a moment. "Well," he said. "I suppose you must be getting on in years. But while you are my sheepdog, you have to earn your keep."

Reluctantly, Herbert rounded up the sheep. When his work was done he found a nice warm spot in the barn and fell fast asleep.

When he woke up, the sun was already high in the sky and the farmer was nowhere to be found. He did not even come to let the sheep out of the pen. Then early in the afternoon he drove back into the yard, opened the back door of the truck – and what should bound out but a handsome young sheepdog.

"Meet the new sheepdog," said the farmer, tickling Herbert in his favorite spot behind the ears. "I think you've earned your retirement. You can sleep in the sun for as long as you like."

loria Lamb's aunt and uncle and her cousin Luke were coming for tea. Gloria's mom had made a delicious chocolate cake.

"When are they coming, Mom?" Gloria asked for the umpteenth time. She couldn't wait to start eating!

At last the doorbell rang. But the grown-ups didn't want to eat right away. They sent Gloria and Luke out to play. Gloria could see the lovely cake through the kitchen window.

"I'm just getting a drink of water," she told Luke as she went into the kitchen.

The chocolate cake looked beautiful.

"Nobody will notice if I eat a tiny piece," Gloria thought. Luke was busy kicking a football about the yard. Gloria broke off the cake and popped it into her mouth. It tasted wonderful. Another bit had come loose, so she ate that too. Then she went back outside.

"Was it good?" asked Luke.

"How did you guess?" Gloria asked in surprise.

"Easy!" said Luke. "You forgot to lick the crumbs off your lips. But I'd have known anyway." He winked. "I always test the cake first when we have visitors!"

**E**veryone on the farm liked Hannah. But her sisters laughed at her because she was skinny.

"You are all white feathers and bone," said Edna.

"It's a pity you're not fat and brown like us," said Harriet as she squeezed into her nest.

One day all three hens were filled with excitement, for they had all laid their very own eggs!

"Oooh, we're going to have baby chicks," said Edna.

"I can't wait," said Harriet.

Hannah smiled to herself and felt her egg beneath her, warm and smooth.

A couple of weeks later, Edna's egg began to crack from the inside – crick, crock, crack. A tiny ball of yellow feathers appeared. Then Harriet's egg started to do the same – crick, crock, crack. A fuzzy yellow ball stepped out. Everyone looked at Hannah and her egg. Nothing happened. They waited. Still nothing happened.

"Perhaps you are too skinny to keep it warm like we can," sniffed Harriet.

Hannah took no notice. She just sat there until a few days later she heard – crick, crock, crack. And out from the egg popped not one but two little chicks. Hannah the skinny hen had twins!

It was almost Christmas, the snow was deep, and the young animals on the farm were very excited.

Their parents were very busy cooking mince pies and wrapping presents so they suggested the youngsters go out sledding.

Katie and Kathryn, the piglets, brought their big sled, and everyone had a wonderful time zooming down the high hill near the woods.

When they'd all had lots of turns, the youngsters set off for home. Just then Ellen the lamb gave a shout.

"Wait a minute," she said, staring at a holly tree with lots of lovely red berries. "Let's put some of this holly on to the sled and take it home to decorate the barn for our Christmas celebrations."

And so they did. When all the animals sat down at the long table in the barn for their Christmas dinner, the grown-ups agreed that they had never seen the barn looking so pretty!

**B**enjamin Piglet was very proud of his curly tail.

"Your tail is completely straight," he said to his friend James Donkey. "It's not pretty and curly like mine."

"My tail is more useful than yours," said James.

Benjamin Piglet laughed. "Don't be silly," he said. "You are just envious."

Just then Wally Wasp flew past. He was feeling tired, so he stopped to have a rest on Benjamin's back. Benjamin tried to shake him off. Wally Wasp got angry, and stung him.

"Ow, ow," shrieked Benjamin. "That hurt!"

Wally Wasp decided to rest somewhere else. This time he landed on the back of James Donkey.

"Let me have a good, comfy sleep," said Wally, "or I'll sting you." But James swished his long, straight tail and knocked Wally off his back. Wally Wasp was so frightened he flew away.

"I told you my straight tail was more useful than your curly one," said James to Benjamin. "And I was right!"

The first thing Mittens did when she was allowed out to explore the barnyard was climb a tree. She loved scrambling up the rough bark. It was wonderful to scratch her neck on the stiff twigs. And the feel of the dappled sunlight warming her fur as she stretched out on a branch was bliss.

One wet day, the kittens were talking about the places they had discovered around the farm.

"My favorite place is the barn," said Blackie. "You can play with the corn and sleep in the straw."

"I like the yard best," said Snowy. "It's fun playing with the chicks."

"The trees are definitely the best place for me," Mittens said. "But I do wish there were more of them."

Just then their mother arrived and heard them.

"Now that you are bigger you can go a little further tomorrow," she smiled. "Blackie can go to the big hay barn in the field. Snowy can try the cowsheds to play with the calves. And Mittens, you can squeeze under the fence by the pond and see what you find."

Next morning, the kittens couldn't wait to explore. Mittens crouched very low and scrambled under the fence, as her mother had told her, to find what from then on was her most favorite place – the orchard!

**T**hey are going to have a special fireworks show at the picnic," Natalie said to Michael. "But if it rains, there'll be no picnic."

"Here comes Uncle Billy Goat," said Michael.

"Are you excited to see the fireworks?" asked Michael.

"Will there be pretty colored ones?" said Natalie.

"Do you think it will rain?" they asked.

"Oh yes," he replied cheerfully. "It will rain!" The twins looked at each other and frowned.

They began to set out the picnic. Billy brought out his special sandwiches, picked some flowers and blew up some balloons. Soon it was dark.

WHOOSH! Suddenly a rocket shot into the air. It burst into stars, and red, yellow and blue stars showered down.

WHIZZ! A green shower came from the next rocket.

"Lovely," cried Natalie.

"Cool!" shouted Michael. The twins agreed it was the best firework show they had ever seen.

**M**rs. Amy Duck had been taking her family of ducklings to the farm pond every day for the past week to practice their swimming.

They were all coming along very well – all except Monty. He refused to get into the water. "I know I'll hate it," he said. "Why must I learn to swim? I'd much rather stay dry."

"All ducks swim," said his mother, who by this time was getting more than a little impatient.

Still Monty refused to put in his foot. Now it happened to be a very windy day, and as he waddled along the side watching his brothers and sisters swimming, a strong gust of wind suddenly got under his feathers, lifted him up and dropped him into the pond!

The water felt soft and silky all around him, and Monty found that his webbed feet were already pushing him quickly towards the others.

"Perhaps I will learn to swim after all!" he giggled.

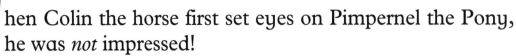

**W**hen Colin the horse first set eyes on Pimpernel the Pony, he was *not* impressed!

"What a funny little thing you are," he said. "Why, your head hardly comes up to my shoulder!"

"Well, you're the size of a mammoth!" retorted Pimpernel. "You and your great shaggy feet!"

So Colin went to one end of the field, and Pimpernel to the other. And that is where they stayed all through the spring! Then came the hot weather, and with the hot weather came – flies! The flies buzzed around Colin at his end of the field, and around Pimpernel at her end.

Both of them flicked at the flies with their tails, but those flies just kept on coming . . .

"One tail isn't enough for all these flies," grumbled Colin, looking down the field at Pimpernel.

"I need some help with these terrible flies," wailed Pimpernel, looking up the field at Colin.

And by the end of the afternoon they were standing together, head to tail, flicking their tails in turn. And they had a lot of talking to catch up on, too!

**P**erry Pig loved to watch the farmer driving his big red tractor. Whenever he heard the noise of the tractor, he peered over the side of his sty.

"I'd love to drive that tractor," he told his friends. "And I'm sure I could. It looks very easy."

"Don't be silly!" they scoffed. "You're a pig. You can't drive tractors!"

One day the farmer drove into the yard – then dashed into the farmhouse, leaving the tractor engine running.

Perry watched it roaring in the yard – suddenly he could bear it no longer. Leaping out of his sty, he ran and jumped up into the cab. As he did so, he knocked a blue lever on the tractor and it began – to move! He was driving!

But Perry's joy quickly turned to horror. The tractor was going straight for the pig sties. And before he could squeak "Help!" it drove smack into the side of his little home. CRASH!

The farmer was furious! "You're a very naughty pig!" he said. "And I can't repair your sty for at least a week." So for a time Perry had nowhere to live. And he decided – very wisely – to leave the driving to the farmer in future.

I t was such a good bone," muttered Patch the farm dog as the mud sprayed up behind his digging feet. "I know I buried it somewhere here. I'll try one more hole . . ." Patch continued to dig. "I wish these flowers were not in the way," he grumbled. But then there was a shout!

"You bad dog!" It was Mrs. Plum, the farmer's wife. "Look at the flowers! I'll have to replant them all."

Patch hid by the barn. He could hear her talking crossly to herself, and when he felt brave enough to peer out from his hiding place he saw that she had replanted the flowers and was going back to the house.

He waited. He waited a bit longer. But he could not resist one last attempt to find his bone. Mud and flowers flew as he dug a really deep hole in the middle of the flower bed. There was something there! Something hard! Was it his bone? No, it was small, hard yellow things, and they tasted – ugh horrible!

"You wicked dog!" Patch was startled and started to run away. "This time I'm going to tie you up and you'll wait a long time until I give you another . . ."

As Mrs. Plum reached the hole, she stopped, bent down, and picked up the shiny things.

"Well, I never," she said. "Old Mr. Plum was right after all. I'd never have believed it, Patch, but you have found treasure! You clever boy!" And, of course, his reward was – a great, big, juicy bone.

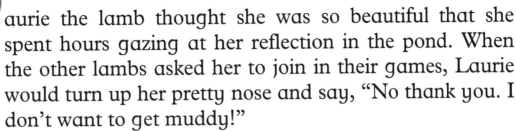

**L**aurie the lamb thought she was so beautiful that she spent hours gazing at her reflection in the pond. When the other lambs asked her to join in their games, Laurie would turn up her pretty nose and say, "No thank you. I don't want to get muddy!"

One day, Laurie was staring at the water when she caught sight of a little white lamb every bit as beautiful as herself, trotting past.

"Hello," said Laurie, spinning round quickly to catch sight of the lamb. But as she turned, she slipped and fell headfirst into the water with a splosh!

Her friends rushed over to see what the noise was about as Laurie pulled herself, dripping, from the pond.

"Oh dear, look at Laurie," said one lamb, finding it hard not to laugh. The others tried not to giggle. Laurie looked at herself in the water – what a sight!

"Aaah," she gasped, but soon even she could not help laughing. "I look like a haystack!" she giggled. At that all the other lambs burst out laughing – and Laurie never wasted her time staring into the water again. It was too much fun playing games.

**A**ll the animals on the farm were enjoying a day trip to the seaside.

Samuel Horse drove their bus, and by eleven o'clock they were all enjoying themselves on the beach. The grown-ups sat in their deck chairs, the puppies chased off into the sea, and the young sheep and kittens built a sand castle. Thomas the donkey gave everyone rides, the calves explored little pools, and the piglets collected shells.

Rebecca Horse had brought two picnic baskets full of delicious things to eat, and after lunch Jessica Pig fetched ice cream for everyone.

But the piglets had collected so many shells they couldn't carry them in their buckets.

"What can we do?" they wailed. "We don't want to leave them behind."

Thomas came to the rescue. "I can carry all sorts of things. Put the shells into the empty picnic baskets and tie them on to my back. I'll carry them up the cliff path to our bus." And he did just that!

**P**atty Pig shared a sty with a much bigger pig named Hattie. They got on very well – apart from one thing. Hattie was very, very greedy!

When dinnertime came, she would rush over and grab all the nicest things – and Patty was left with just the potato peelings.

"It's not fair that you grab the best things all the time," Patty grumbled.

"I'm a bigger pig," boomed Hattie. "And I need more food. It's **quite** fair!"

One day the pigs' dinner came – topped with glistening red jam!

"Jam!" roared Hattie and, pushing Patty aside as usual, she started gobbling it up.

But in her greed Hattie didn't notice something. Sitting on the strawberry jam was a large striped wasp – which promptly stung her on the snout!

"Ow, ow, ow!" screamed Hattie.

"Serves you right for being so greedy," said the other farm animals.

After that Hattie always let Patty have **some** of the nicer things!

**C**an we play with Rosie?" Dick asked his father.

"I don't think so," he said. "You know she's a nuisance. We named her Rosie because she ate my roses."

"Please, Dad," begged Dick and his sister Linda.

"Oh, all right then," said the farmer. "But don't let that goat near my roses."

The children took Rosie into the garden. Linda stroked her soft white fur while Dick played with her grizzly white beard.

"She's a sweet goat. Dad is wrong to think she's greedy," said Dick. "I don't think she's a nuisance!"

Soon the children tired of playing with her. They lay on the lawn and made daisy chains. Rosie wandered off. She saw the farmer's rose bushes.

"Delicious," she bleated and hurried over to them. Crunch . . . munch . . . Rosie gobbled up the red roses. Then she ate the yellow roses. Then she ate the pink roses! Suddenly Dick noticed Rosie was missing.

"She was here a minute ago!" said Linda.

When Dad returned from the milking, he saw Rosie in the garden – with the very last pink rose in her mouth!

"Dick! Linda!" he shouted, but they were nowhere to be found. They hid in the shed until he calmed down. But he never let them play with Rosie again.

he white doves hadn't lived on the farm for long. The farmer had built them a wooden house – called the dovecote – high on the roof of the barn.

Once a week a van came to the farm delivering special cattle food to the farmer, and the doves saw a way of making friends with the other animals. As soon as they saw the van in the distance, they flew down to the cows and said, "The man with your food is on his way. Hurry across the field to the trough where the farmer puts it."

The cows set off, one following the other, so that by the time the farmer reached the trough, they were waiting for him – week after week, after week.

"Do you know," the farmer said to his wife, "our cows are so clever, they even seem to know which day of the week their special food arrives."

And from that day on, the doves became part of the happy barnyard family!

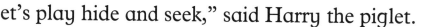

"L et's play hide and seek," said Harry the piglet.

"Okay," agreed his sister Debbie. "Who will hide?"

"I will," announced Harry. "Shut your eyes and count to ten – and no peeking!"

"You are the one who peeks," answered Debbie crossly. "I never peek." *One, two three* . . .

Harry wondered where to go. He looked around the barnyard. Behind the milk churn? No, she would look there first. *Four, five, six* . . . Under the hen coop? No, the hens would squawk. *Seven, eight, nine* . . .

"I know," he decided. "I'll hide in the barn. It will be nice and warm in there." He dashed into the barn just as Debbie shouted, "*Ten!* Ready or not, here I come."

Suddenly a gust of wind blew the door shut with a BANG! Harry was trapped. It was dark. Something rustled in the straw. He felt frightened. Debbie would never find him here.

"Harry!" It was Debbie's voice. Where was she? "There's a loose plank here," she said. Harry could see a chink of light. Puffing and pushing with all his might he was soon free.

"Thank you," smiled Harry. Debbie looked downcast.

"I peeked," she admitted.

"Never mind," said Harry. "I'm very glad you did!"

**N**ell, the old horse, was telling her great-granddaughter, Juniper, all about the days when she had pulled the plough and the hay cart on the farm. The foal had only ever seen the tractor do this.

"Oh, please tell me about the lovely harness you wore, and the ribbons," she begged. So Nell told her all over again.

"I wish I could have seen how you looked," Juniper sighed. "Just be patient," said Nell, smiling a secret smile.

Every summer, the farmer and his family organized a village show in the field near the stream. Juniper watched in amazement as Nell was brushed till her coat shone. Jingling harness and horse bells were put on her, and her mane and tail were plaited with red and blue ribbons. She even had little red caps over her ears to keep the flies away.

And no one was prouder than Juniper as she watched Nell pull a lovely old hay cart into the show ring!

The animals were so excited. Their favorite day of the year had almost arrived. The posters had been put up weeks before. The sheds had been tidied and the gates mended. The only trouble was that the young animals had no idea what was going on.

"Please tell us," they begged, but the reply was always the same, "Be patient! It's worth waiting for."

Peter Puppy tried to hide in the straw and listen to the horses, but he sneezed and they shooed him away.

Albert Chick felt sure he would hear something when he hid under the leaves by the ducks' pond, but they only talked about whose feathers were the loveliest.

Melissa Mouse thought she had a better chance than anyone to creep up on the grown-ups and hear some news, but Tom Cat kept a beady, watchful eye on her all the time.

When the day finally came, the excitement was almost too much to bear.

"Ready, team?" said Farmer Chris as he pulled back the big farm gates. There was a chorus of happy noises from all of the animals as a steady stream of children and their families came in to look around the farm and to stroke and pet and feed the animals. And the young ones agreed that it was definitely worth waiting for!

**B**etty Bat was flying around the farm at night. She had been asleep all day, but now she thought she would like to visit her friends. It was a very windy night, and all the trees were swaying and shaking their branches.

Betty flew to the top of the tree where Cindy Sparrow lived. But her nest was no longer there. It had been blown out of the tree by the wind.

"Oh, what am I going to do?" cried Cindy Sparrow. "I have nowhere to live."

"Don't worry," said Betty Bat. "You can come home with me tonight." Cindy Sparrow was still frightened.

"Won't the wind blow your nest down too?" she asked. Betty Bat just laughed.

She took her friend back to the barn where she lived. They flew high up to the beams beneath the roof.

"We'll be safe here," said Betty Bat.

So Betty Bat hung upside down on the beam, and Cindy Sparrow sat beside her.

The wind whistled and roared, but it didn't worry them one bit!

One evening Penelope Pig was lying on her back looking at the moon.

"I wonder what it could be," she thought. So she asked Milly the cow.

"Milly, I've been wondering – what is the moon?"

"Oh, that's simple," Milly replied. 'The moon is a huge bucket of milk."

To Penelope this seemed a little strange so she asked Shirley the sheep.

"Shirley, can you tell me what the moon is?"

"Easy," said Shirley. "It's a giant white fleece."

Now Penelope was really confused so she asked Sophie the hen.

"Sophie, do you know what the moon is?"

"It's obvious, isn't it?" Sophie replied. "It is an enormous white egg."

By now Penelope did not know what to think, so she told her mother what everyone had said.

"But who is telling the truth?" she asked.

"They are all telling the truth," smiled her mother. "Since none of us really know what the moon is, it can be whatever we want it to be."

What would you like the moon to be?

**L**et's start our own band – then we can play exciting music," said Libby Lamb.

"Don't be silly," said her friend Simon Calf. "How can we play music without instruments?"

"We can make our own," she said. Libby jumped on top of an old oil drum and danced around, making a loud drumming noise. Then she jumped onto a smaller drum next to it that made a different sound. "There," she said. "I'm the drummer."

"You can blow these," said Libby, pointing excitedly to some plastic water pipes that had been left in the barnyard. Simon huffed and puffed and at last managed to make some sounds.

"What's all that noise?" asked Henry Hedgehog, rustling through the dry leaves under the hedge.

"Hey, that sounds great!" laughed Libby. "Come and join our band."

"This looks like fun," said Gerald Goat. "Can I play the guitar?" And he started to pluck the wire fence where it ran past the wooden barn.

What a wonderful time they all had drumming, blowing, rustling and plucking!

"I think we are so good," announced Libby, "that *we* ought to make a record!"

Jemima, the old tabby farm cat, was sitting on the barn-yard wall with her kittens.

"Tonight's bath night, so I'm going to teach you how to wash yourselves," she said. "Cats like to be clean but it takes a bit of practice. Come down off the wall and I'll show you how to do it."

Three of the kittens jumped down after their mother, but the fourth, Terry, had other ideas. He'd seen two birds splashing about in a puddle taking a bath. "That looks like much more fun. I think I'll try that."

He leaped off the wall, ran towards the puddle and jumped in with a splash. "Oh, it's horrible," he squealed. "My fur is all wet and my tail is soggy!"

From the entrance to the barn his mother and brothers laughed. "You'd better leave water to the birds," Jemima said. "Cats don't like to get wet. Now shake the water off your paws, come here and I'll start the lesson again!"

**L**eyla and Esther, the rabbit twins, were a little nervous about starting school. They had often seen the school teacher, Mrs. Turkey, in the barnyard. She was stout with beady eyes that never missed anything.

When Esther was teasing Leyla that she could not hop nearly as far as she could, Mrs. Turkey stopped and turned her wrinkled neck to look at Esther – very crossly.

When Leyla was jumping in the puddles and splashing everyone, Mrs. Turkey stopped and turned her wrinkled neck to look at Leyla – very crossly indeed.

"I think those beady eyes only know how to look cross," said Esther as the twins hopped slowly across the yard and into the schoolroom in the barn.

"Or very cross indeed," added Leyla.

All the other animals were arriving at the same time. Mrs. Turkey was sitting in the corner, quietly writing. As each one came in, she turned her wrinkled neck to look at them – very kindly indeed.

"Hello class," she said with a big smile. "You all know me, I'm Mrs. Turkey. And I think we are going to get along just fine." And do you know, she was right!

Scott the rabbit had a new ball. It was bright red, and it was *very* bouncy. He could not wait to show all of his friends how bouncy it was. He bounced it on the ground. It flew up and hit the barn, waking the hen.

"Go and play with your ball somewhere else," she squawked. "You woke me up!"

He hopped to the other side of the barnyard and bounced it again. It flew even higher and bounced down on the back of the grumpy old goat.

"Go and play with your ball somewhere else," he grumbled. "That hurt!"

"Bother," said Scott. He took his ball to the edge of the barnyard. This time he bounced it so high that it bounced and bounced and – vanished over the barnyard wall. Scott scurried under the fence and looked around. He could not see his ball anywhere. He hopped a little further and looked around – but still no ball.

Then he looked up. He could not believe his eyes! Wherever he looked, the trees were covered in red balls.

"How will I ever find mine?" he wailed. Then Sarah Squirrel's face peered out from between the branches.

"You silly rabbit," she laughed. "These are apples! Try looking on the ground." And, sure enough, that was where Scott found his bright red ball.

George Cat lived on the farm. Every night at bedtime he went around to check that all the animals were safe.

"Silly old George," said Mrs. Hen. "He thinks he's a guard dog."

George even visited Boris Bull, who was so fierce he had to live in a field on his own.

One night, George was keeping watch as usual. He went to see Gregory Goat.

"Everything all right?" he asked.

"Yes, thank you," said Gregory.

He went to visit Mrs. Hen in her coop, even though she sometimes made fun of him.

"Everything all right?" he started to ask.

But everything wasn't all right. The lock on the hen house door was broken. Fergus Fox was trying to get in. George ran back to the farmhouse and jumped through the open window.

"Meow, meow, meow," he said loudly. He woke up the farmer, who chased Fergus Fox away.

"Thank you for saving me and my chicks," said Mrs. Hen. "You really are as brave as a guard dog."

And she never made fun of George Cat again.

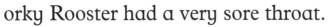orky Rooster had a very sore throat.

"You must rest your voice," said David Donkey.

"Tomorrow morning I have to sit on the cowshed roof and crow," said Corky. "All the animals depend on me to wake them up."

"Somebody must do it for you," said David. So Corky Rooster's friends lined up to have a try.

Mrs. Hen flew on to the cowshed roof and went, "Cluck, cluck."

"Not loud enough," said Corky.

Mrs. Goose had a turn.

"Honk, honk," went Mrs. Goose.

"Far too quiet," said Corky.

Mrs. Turkey took her place on the cowshed roof.

"Gobble, gobble," went Mrs. Turkey.

"I can't hear you," said Corky Rooster.

Corky was worried. What could he do now?

David Donkey said, "Let me have a try."

"You can't climb on the cowshed roof," said Corky.

But David threw back his head and went, "Hee-haw, hee-haw." It was so loud that all the animals heard him, even those in the nearby fields.

"Just think what it would be like if I climbed on the cowshed roof!" said David proudly.

op and Skip, the twin white goats, hated bath night. Every time their mother called them in they made hundreds of excuses.

"I can't have a bath tonight," Hop said. "I've got my homework to do."

"I've still got a bandage on my knee from when I fell off my bike," said Skip. "It will come off in the bath."

Their mother had had enough of excuses and into the bath they went. As it was a warm summer's evening she said that they could go outside to dry off before bed. The bath had made their coats silky and soft.

"Oh, you look lovely," said Kitty the calf. "Your fur is so white."

Tim the turkey waddled over. "You both look so nice and clean!"

Then Ronald the robin, who lived in an old watering can in the corner of the barn, flew down, crying, "I've never seen your coats so silky." Hop and Skip blushed.

"Perhaps baths aren't so bad!" they laughed.

**S**oon it would be Carol the calf's birthday. She wrote invitations to her party and gave them to her friends. She learned a song to sing to them, as a surprise.

Her friends brought her some lovely presents: a paintbox, a book, a box of chocolates, and a necklace.

They ate in the garden – oatmeal cookies, cinnamon buns, jelly donuts, and ice cream. Carol blew out her candles in one big poof! Then they played hide and seek and charades. Then Carol sang her surprise song.

When she'd finished, everybody clapped. Carol's friends had planned some surprises too. Perky did a dance while Christine played her harmonica. Bert played a tune on his recorder. The others sang a song and the neighbors opened their windows and joined in the chorus.

"Wasn't I lucky, Mom?" Carol said after her friends had gone home. "I always have a party, but this year was really special. I had a Carol concert!"

**I** want to fly!" said Marigold to her friend Polly the pig.

"Hens can't fly very far," said Polly.

"But I want to fly over the moon and over the stars!" said Marigold.

"A cow jumped over the moon once," mooed Henrietta the cow, thoughtfully.

Marigold flapped her short brown wings but she only managed to flutter up to the lowest branches of a tree.

"If I could get to the top of the tree," she said, "and jump off, then I might reach the moon!"

Oliver the cat was sleeping in the branches of the tree.

"Oliver, I want to get to the top," she said.

"Then climb aboard, my friend," smiled Oliver. "I'll take you!"

Marigold reached the top of the tree. "Uh, oh!" she said. The ground looked so far away it made her dizzy. But she was determined.

"Wheeeee!" she yelled as she jumped off. She tried to go upwards but . . . down . . . down . . . down she went until . . . Plonk! she landed on Polly's head.

"I don't want a hen as a hat!" giggled Polly.

"Well!" clucked Marigold. She had lost a few feathers but otherwise only her pride was hurt. "In the future I will stick to the ground!"

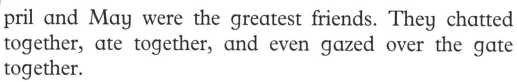

April and May were the greatest friends. They chatted together, ate together, and even gazed over the gate together.

Once, however, they had a fight. They were grazing as usual, when suddenly – at the same time – they spotted something in the grass. It was a lucky four-leaf clover!

"Mine, I think," said April, picking it up neatly with her teeth.

"I think *not*," said May angrily. "I saw it first!"

"Well, it seems as though *I* have it," said April out of the corner of her mouth.

"Only because you grabbed it!" said May. And she was so cross she reached over, and snatched the four-leaf clover with her teeth. April hung on tight – and between them the four-leaf clover was torn in two!

They looked at each other in horror – then suddenly burst out laughing. They both looked so silly.

"Let's not ruin our friendship over one silly little plant," said May.

"No!" said April. "We can share the luck between us!"

**D**ominick, the farmer's son, kept Clover and Nutmeg, his black and white rabbits, in a hutch by the farmhouse. He fed them juicy lettuce, cabbage and dandelion leaves every day, and when he came home from school he let them have a run in a big pen he had made.

Some wild rabbits lived in a high bank not far away, and one night, when everyone was asleep, they crept up to the hutches.

"Why don't you bite your way through the netting on your hutch and come and live with us?" they said to the two rabbits. "We're not locked up. We're free."

Clover and Nutmeg looked at each other. "But we have a warm house with clean straw to lie in," Clover said. "William brings us our food, and we have a run every day. I don't think we'd be very good at looking after ourselves."

"You go back to your burrows and we'll stay here," said Nutmeg. "We're very comfortable, thank you!"

**I**t was a hot, clear day. Excitement filled the center court for the mixed doubles final. The annual Farm Tennis Tournament was a great event every year.

As Porky the pig and Feather the chicken strode confidently onto the court, the crowd cheered. They were sure to win. Then came Starlight the horse and Denise the cow. Their friends had to cheer especially loudly because there weren't many of them.

"Will the audience please go to their seats," Mr. Pig announced. "The game will begin in five minutes."

The first set was easy. Porky was famous for his tricks and Feather for her speed. They looked at each other proudly and held their noses in the air. They were sure to win.

But Starlight and Denise soon began to play better. They were enjoying themselves. Porky and Feather began to make mistakes. Porky hit too heavily and the ball flew off the court. Feather hit too lightly and it did not go over the net.

It was a nail-biting finish, but Starlight and Denise were declared the new champions, which just goes to show that no one is *sure* to win.

# LAURA AND THE SPIDER

One day Laura Lamb and Donny Ram were playing hide and seek in the field. Laura ran into some bushes to hide. She had found such a good hiding place, and she kept so very still, that Donny could not find her.

"Laura, Laura," he bleated, but Laura had gone to sleep and did not hear him!

Suddenly, she awoke with a start. Something was tickling her nose. She froze. She did not dare move. She lay there very, very still and the thing went on tickling her nose.

Meanwhile, Donny had gone to tell the others that Laura was missing. Soon they were all searching.

"Laura, come baaack," they called.

"Baa, I'm here," she bleated, keeping as still as she could. Her mother barged through the bushes.

"Whatever are you doing?" she asked.

"I can't move," whispered Laura. "There's something on my nose." Her mom laughed.

"You silly lamb. It's only a spider making a web. You stayed still for so long she must have thought you were part of the bush. Come on, now. It's time to go home for dinner. The spider will have to start again."

artha loved to sing. She knew all the songs that played on the radio in the milking shed. But the other cows weren't interested in listening to her. They preferred munching grass all day. Martha needed an audience, so she wandered around the farm looking for someone who would appreciate her talents.

Passing the duck pond she noticed some activity in among the reeds. There she found several frogs croaking away to one of her favorite songs, and she started to sing along with them. Martha sang as loud as she could and the frogs joined in with all the choruses. Soon a big crowd of farm animals had gathered around the pond and were clapping along with Martha's performance.

"What's going on?" asked the other cows, who had walked over to see where the noise was coming from.

"It's a new band," shouted the ducks. "They are called Martha and the Croakettes!"

**T**he first animal to wake in the barnyard was always Roland Rooster. The first thing he did was climb onto a haystack, open his beak – and wake everyone else up! His "cock-a-doodle-doo" was the loudest in the village.

The animals all grumbled about Roland's crowing.

"That noise goes right through me," said Wilbur Pig.

"It really frightens me," said Fiona Horse.

"I was having a lovely dream this morning," said Sylvia Sheep, "until Roland's crowing ruined it."

One day, however, Roland had a sore throat and couldn't crow in the morning. So everyone overslept.

Wilbur was behind all day with his work, the farmer was late with Fiona's oats and, because she slept so late, Sylvia's dream turned into a nightmare!

It didn't take long for the animals to change their mind about Roland.

"I hope your voice gets better soon," they told him. "We don't like being awakened so early – but it's better than NOT being awakened at all!"

Helen the deer's grandma was coming to visit.

"I'll gather some flowers to put in grandma's room," Helen thought.

There were lots of pretty flowers growing in the fields near Helen's home – bluebells, buttercups and daisies. But at the bottom of the field near a stream, she noticed some golden-yellow flowers which looked prettier than all the rest.

"I must have some of those," Helen thought.

She ran through the long, damp grass to where they were growing. But the ground was so soft and squishy near the river, that her feet began to sink in the mud. Poor Helen felt very frightened!

As she sank deeper, Helen grabbed at a bush to save herself. Still hanging on, she stretched out and reached the golden flowers and picked a precious few. Then she managed to pull herself out of the mud. She was a mess! But she was very pleased with the flowers.

When she got home she put the flowers in a little jug. They looked so beautiful that she almost forgot how frightened she had felt when she sank in the mud. But when she looked at her feet she remembered! She would not pick those flowers again no matter how beautiful they were. And she rushed off to wash her feet before Grandma arrived.